Easter Bunny Baby

by Sarah Willson

illustrated by Sharon Ross and Kevin Gallegly

SCHOLASTIC INC.

New York   Toronto   London   Auckland   Sydney
Mexico City   New Delhi   Hong Kong   Buenos Aires

D1275531

KLASKY CSUPO INC.

Based on the TV series *Rugrats*® created by Arlene Klasky, Gabor Csupo, and Paul Germain as seen on Nickelodeon®

ISBN 0-439-59883-4

12 11 10 9 8 7 6 5 4 3 2 1   4 5 6 7 8 9/0

Printed in the U.S.A.

First Scholastic printing, January 2004

"And don't forget," Angelica was telling the Easter Bunny, "I want lotsa jelly beans and licor-icor-ish. And lighten up on those marshmallow chickies. I need more chocolate eggs. And oh, yeah. . . ."

The Easter Bunny groaned. "I have a headache," he said. "I'm going to take a long break."

"Oh, dear," said Didi. "It looks like the Easter Bunny isn't feeling well."

"What a shame," said Kira. "I was looking forward to having a nice Easter photo of the children."

"Did you hear that?" asked Tommy. "The Easter Bunny is sick!"

"I'm a little ascared of the Easter Bunny anyway," said Chuckie, "and the marshmallow chicks, too."

Just then Kimi had a thought. "Hey, you guys, what if the Easter Bunny is too sick to bring us our Easter baskets tomorrow?"

Suddenly they were all speechless—even Angelica.

That night Chuckie was worried. "Kimi! What if the Easter Bunny really doesn't come tomorrow? Kimi?" But Kimi was fast asleep.

Chuckie sighed and turned over. "Yipes!" He quickly reached for his glasses. The Easter Bunny was standing right in front of him!

"Ch-Chuckie!" gasped the Easter Bunny, clutching his stomach. "You gotta—cough!—help me. You gotta finish—cough! cough!—delivering these Easter baskets for—cough!—me. They're for Tommy, and Phil, and Lil—"

Chuckie didn't need to hear any more. "I gots to be brave," he muttered. Chuckie loaded the baskets into his ridey-car. "Okay, Easter Bunny," he said. "My friends can count on me!"

Then he grabbed Kimi. "Come on, Kimi," he said, "we gots a job to do!"

"Chuckie, look!" said Kimi, pointing. A gang of giant chickens had suddenly appeared!

"Not so fast!" said one chicken. "Give us back our eggs!"

"Drive, Chuckie, drive!" yelled the Easter Bunny.

Chuckie drove.

"Those giant chickens aren't going to get these baskets!" said Kimi. She pulled a handful of jellybeans out of a basket and tossed them on the ground. The chickens started to slip and slide, their wings flapping wildly.

"Good work, Kimi," said Chuckie, pedaling hard. "We're almost at Phil and Lil's . . . AAAAH!!!"

The car sailed over a hill . . .

crashed into a huge pile of
Easter grass . . .

and tossed Chuckie and Kimi out onto a bed of sand.

"It's no use," Chuckie said as they crawled toward Phil and
Lil's house. "We'll never get these delivered in time."

"So . . . thirsty . . ." said Kimi.

And then they heard a familiar bark. "Woof! Woof! Woof!"

"Spike!" yelled Chuckie.

Spike had brought them sippy cups of milk! After drinking the milk Chuckie and Kimi felt a lot better. They ran the rest of the way to Phil and Lil's house.

"That takes care of the first two Easter baskets," said Chuckie. "We have four more to go."

"Hey, there's Susie's house," Kimi said as they were walking through a huge field. Just then they noticed a group of lambs bounding toward them.

"Argh!" cried Chuckie as he and Kimi started to run.

"Head for that fence!" Kimi shouted.

"Make like a snake, Kimi!" Chuckie yelled. They both dropped down onto their bellies and shimmied under the fence.

"Whew! That was close!" Kimi said. They hurried to Susie's house.

"Three delivered, three to go," said Chuckie after dropping off Susie's basket. Then he noticed the river of chocolate—and Angelica's house on the other side.

"We gots to make our way across, Kimi," he said.

"Mmm . . . this river is yummy," Kimi said, tasting the chocolate.

"We gots to keep moving, Kimi," said Chuckie.

After a while they made it across. But two baskets got caught in the current. "We gots to get them!" Chuckie yelled. He reached into a basket he was holding and pulled out two strands of licorice. Then they lassoed each basket and reeled them in.

Chuckie and Kimi lifted Angelica's basket onto her front stoop.

"Looks like the Easter Bunny gave Angelica everything she asked for," said Chuckie, panting.

He picked up the last two Easter baskets. "These are for Tommy and Dil."

"Uh, Chuckie, do you hear something?" asked Kimi.

Chuckie and Kimi looked up. Coming over the hill was a long line of marshmallow chicks!

"Run, Chuckie, run!" yelled Kimi as she started to run. "I can't!" Chuckie yelled back. His feet felt heavy. He couldn't move, no matter how hard he tried.

Peeeep! Peeeep!

Chuckie watched Kimi run up to the Pickles' front stoop just as Tommy opened the door. Kimi dashed inside to safety. But Chuckie's feet still wouldn't move.

"Well, the Easter Bunny came through this year!" she said excitedly. "I gots tons of chocolates and jellybeans and licor-icor-ish. And he only gave me one of these dumb marshmallow chicks. Here, you can have it, Finster."

"No! Chuckie's ascared of these!" Kimi said.

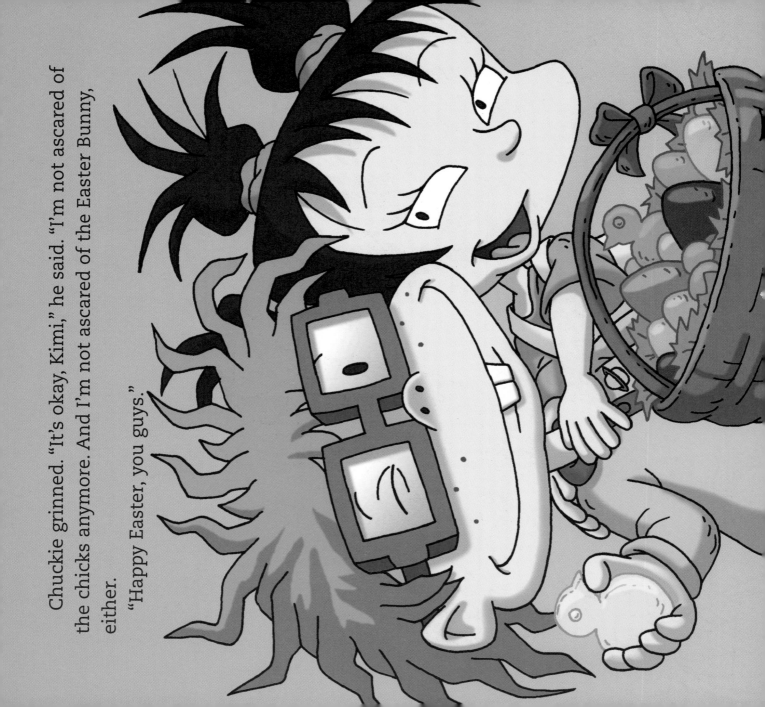

Chuckie grinned. "It's okay, Kimi," he said. "I'm not ascared of the chicks anymore. And I'm not ascared of the Easter Bunny, either.

"Happy Easter, you guys."

Finally he hurled the two Easter baskets toward Tommy. "Catch, Tommy!" he cried. He watched them sail through the air as the marshmallow chicks closed in on him.

"You gots to catch those baskets, Tommy! Tommy . . . Tommy . . . Tommy. . . ."

"Hey, Chuckie, wake up!" Tommy said. "The Easter Bunny got well and brought us our Easter baskets! Look, here's yours." Chuckie opened his eyes and reached for his glasses just as Angelica came barging in.